THE
ABC
BUNNY

THE ABC BUNNY

By **WANDA GÁG**

HAND LETTERED BY HOWARD GÁG

PUBLISHED IN NEW YORK BY
COWARD–McCANN, INC.

L.C. number: 33-27359
ISBN 0-698-20000-4 (hardcover edition)
30   29   28
First paperback edition published October 1978
ISBN 0-698-20465-4 (paperback edition)
10   9   8   7   6

for Apple, big and red

B

for Bunny snug a-bed

C for Crash!

D for Dash!

E

for Elsewhere in a flash

F for Frog – he's fat and funny

"Looks like rain," says he to Bunny

G for Gale !

H for Hail !

Hippy-hop goes Bunny's tail

I

for Insects here and there

J

for Jay with jaunty air

K

for Kitten , catnip-crazy

L

for Lizard – look how lazy

M

for Mealtime – munch , munch , munch

M-m-m! these greens are good for lunch

N

for Napping in a Nook

O

for Owl with bookish look

P

for prickly Porcupine

J

for Jay with jaunty air

K

for Kitten , catnip-crazy

L

for Lizard – look how lazy

M

for Mealtime – munch , munch , munch

M-m-m! these greens are good for lunch

N

for Napping in a Nook

O

for Owl with bookish look

P

for prickly Porcupine

Pins and needles on his spine

Q for Quail

R for Rail

S

for Squirrel Swishy-tail

T

for Tripping back to Town

U

for Up and Up-side-down

V for View

Valley too

W

—"We welcome you!"

for eXit – off, away!

That's enough for us today

Y

for You, take one last look

Z

for Zero – close the book!